Max
the Brave

by Ed Vere

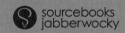
sourcebooks
jabberwocky

This is Max.

Doesn't Max look sweet?

Max looks so sweet that sometimes
people dress him up with bows.

Max does **not** like being
dressed up with bows.

Because Max is a fearless kitten.

Max is a brave kitten.

Max is a kitten who chases **mice**.

Max the Brave just needs to find out
what a mouse looks like. . .

and then he will chase it.

Maybe Mouse is in there.

Max bravely explores the can.
"Mouse? Are you in there?"

Hmmm, Mouse isn't here.

Oh, hello. . .

"Are **you** Mouse?"

"No, I'm Fly," says Fly. "But I just saw
Mouse scurry by a moment ago."

Hmmm, maybe this is
what Mouse looks like.

"Excuse me, please,
but are **you** Mouse?"

"I'm not Mouse. I'm Fish," says Fish.
"But I just saw Mouse dash outside."

That **must** be Mouse,
up in the tree.

"Excuse me, please, but are **you** Mouse?"

"We are not Mouse. We are birds," say the birds.

"But we did just see Mouse scoot by."

"Excuse me, but would **you**
happen to be Mouse?"

"Eeek, Mouse?!
I'm not Mouse. I'm Elephant,"
says Elephant.
"But I did just see Mouse skitter by."

"Thank you very much,"
says Max.

"And **you**?"

"Nope. . .thattaway."

"Hello there. Are **you** Mouse by any chance?"

"Who, **me**? No, certainly not.

I'm Monster!"

squeaks Mouse. "But I did just see

Mouse asleep over there. . .

If you're very quick, you might catch him."

"Thank you very much," says Max.

This **must** be Mouse.

Hmmm, I didn't know Mouse was so BIG.

"Ahem, excuse me, **Mouse**, will you wake up please?

I am Max the Brave,

and I have come to chase **you**."

"Wakey, wakey, Mouse!"

yells Max as he bounces up and down
on Monster's head.

"I am Max the Brave, and I chase mice!
And I might just eat you up too!"

Hmmm, I didn't know Mouse had such BIG teeth.

GULP!

ATTCHOOO!!

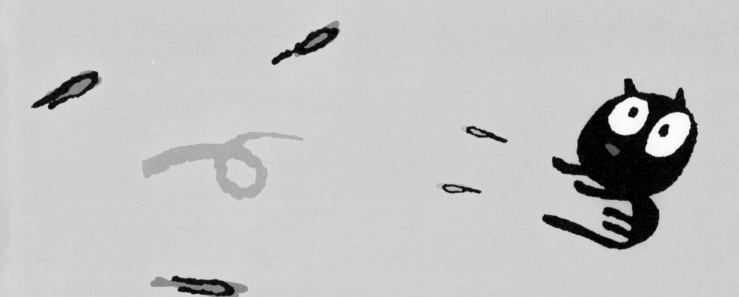

"Yuck!"

Max decides that chasing mice

is not all it's cracked up to be.

And anyway, he doesn't need to be
Max the Brave all the time. . .

Unless he's out chasing. . .

. . .monsters.

for
gatita

Copyright © 2015 by Ed Vere
Cover images/illustrations © Ed Vere

Sourcebooks and the colophon are registered trademarks of Sourcebooks, Inc.
All rights reserved. No part of this book may be reproduced in any form or by any electronic or mechanical means including information
storage and retrieval systems—except in the case of brief quotations embodied in critical articles or reviews—without permission in
writing from its publisher, Sourcebooks, Inc.
Published by Sourcebooks Jabberwocky, an imprint of Sourcebooks, Inc.
P.O. Box 4410, Naperville, Illinois 60567-4410
(630) 961-3900
Fax: (630) 961-2168
www.sourcebooks.com
Originally published in 2014 in the United Kingdom by Puffin Books, an imprint of Penguin Random House.
Library of Congress Cataloging-in-Publication data in on file with the publisher.
Source of Production: South China Printing Co. Ltd, Millenium City, Kowloon, Hong Kong
Date of Production: March 2015
Printed and bound in China.
10 9 8 7 6 5 4 3 2